ADDY'S CUP OF SUGAR

Based on the Buddhist Story "The Mustard Seed"

A Stillwater Tale by JON J MUTH

SCHOLASTIC PRESS / NEW YORK

Thank you to Ashokan, Hex, and Jinx,
our most excellent feline friends!

LIBRARY OF CONGRESS CATALOGING-IN-PUBLICATION DATA
Names: Muth, Jon J, author, illustrator.
Title: Addy's cup of sugar / by Jon J Muth.
Description: First edition. | New York : Scholastic Press, 2020. | "From the original Buddhist story, 'Kisa Gotami and the The Mustard Seed.'" Summary: In this reworking of the Buddhist parable, Stillwater, a giant panda, teaches Addy that the grief she feels for the loss of her kitten is part of life and is shared by everybody.
Identifiers: LCCN 2019035958 | ISBN 9780439634281 (hardback)
Subjects: LCSH: Children and death—Juvenile fiction. | Grief—Juvenile fiction. | Buddhist parables—Juvenile fiction. | CYAC: Death—Fiction. | Grief—Fiction. | Giant panda—Fiction. | Pandas—Fiction. | LCGFT: Parables.
Classification: LCC PZ7.M97274 Ad 2020 | DDC [E]—dc23 LC record available at https://lccn.loc gov/2019035958

10 9 8 7 6 5 4 3 2 1 20 21 22 23 24
Printed in China 38
First edition, October 2020

Jon J Muth's main source for this story is "Kisa Gotami: There Is No Cure for Death," in *Buddhist Parables*, translated by Eugene Watson Burlingame (New Haven: Yale University Press, 1922), 92–94.

Jon J Muth's drawings were created with watercolor and pencil on d'Arches paper.
The type was set in Monotype Fournier.
The book was printed on 150 gsm Lumisilk matt art paper and bound at Tien Wah Press.
Production was overseen by Catherine Weening. Manufacturing was supervised by Shannon Rice.
The book was art directed and designed by David Saylor and Charles Kreloff, and edited by Dianne Hess.

For Molly

For Addy

Addy and her pet kitten were best friends.

They did everything together.

When he was very young, his meow sounded like the tooting of a tiny brass horn.

Addy named him Trumpet.

They woke up together every day.

Trumpet sat on the covers and wouldn't move until Addy got out of bed.

When Trumpet was with her, the world was brighter and warmer.

But one day, shortly after they moved into their new neighborhood, it happened.

Trumpet was hit by a car.

Addy was very sad.
Trumpet couldn't be gone.
This couldn't really be happening.
There must be something she could do!

Then Addy remembered her friend Stillwater. He knew a lot about how to help people. He would know how to bring Trumpet back again.

Addy ran to find him.

"Stillwater! Stillwater!" Addy cried out.
"You have to help make Trumpet alive again!
Please make him come back!"

"Oh, Addy," Stillwater said softly, "I am so sorry.

"Perhaps we can find the medicine you need.

"But first you will need all the right ingredients. You must go around the neighborhood and find someone to give you a cup of sugar."

Stillwater handed Addy an empty cup.

"Fill this cup with sugar and bring it to me so we can mix it into the right medicine.

"But the most important thing of all is that the sugar *must* be from a home where death is a stranger."

Addy hurried outside.

She ran as fast as she could to the nearest house.

Emma, who was visiting her grandmother, answered the door. "Do you have a cup of sugar I could have?" asked Addy.

"Yes, I'm sure we do," Emma said.

"Oh good," said Addy. "Stillwater needs it for a special medicine."

Then Addy remembered. "Does anybody in your family know someone who has died?"

"My grandpa died last year," said Emma.

"Oh," said Addy, unsure of what to say next. "I'm sorry about your grandpa. But the sugar for this medicine must be from a home where no one has died. I'm sorry to bother you," she said.

Addy ran through the backyards and beneath the laundry that hung on clotheslines. The linen sheets that brushed against her skin felt like Trumpet's rough tongue.

She never knew what a cat's tongue felt like until she met Trumpet.

Addy went to another house and knocked. She was surprised when her school librarian answered the door. “Please,” said Addy. “I’m helping my friend Stillwater make a special medicine.

“I need to find a cup of sugar, but it must be from a home where no one has died.”

“I’m sorry,” said the librarian quietly. “Last week our dear old dog, Gracie, died in her sleep. I wish I could be of more help.”

"Oh," said Addy, as quiet as the librarian. "That's okay. Thank you. And I'm sorry about your Gracie."

Addy ran from neighbor to neighbor looking for a cup of sugar from a home where death was a stranger. But she couldn't find a single one.

Each person had, at one time or another, lost someone who was dear to them.

Knowing she had to hurry, Addy scampered across the yard through some bushes between the trees.

A rabbit watched her run past, the pupils in his eyes growing so very large. It was like when Trumpet would sit very still, and watch, and wait — then he would pounce!

"Ouch!" Addy's pants leg caught on a sticker bush. A sharp thorn broke the skin on her knee. She sat down and unhooked the thorn.

"I'm sorry, Trumpet!" Addy said. "I am trying to help you as quickly as I can."

Addy thought about all the people she had met today.

When she looked at their faces, she knew how each of them had felt. And while she was still very sad, she did not feel quite so alone.

She thought of Trumpet. Of how he chased dragonflies in the yard. How she would find him curled up asleep in the funniest places. How his little pink toes felt so soft. How he would purr and rub his chin against her cheek while she lay in the grass looking at the clouds.

Now she felt the tears come.

The light was chasing the end of the day.

After a long moment watching the sky, Addy stood and began to run.

Stillwater was waiting for her on the porch.

"I have no sugar, Stillwater," Addy said. "Everyone I met today has lost someone they love.

"But I understand now," she said.
"The medicine was for me, wasn't it?"

Stillwater smiled a beautiful sad smile.

"How will I ever stop being sad about Trumpet?" asked Addy.

Stillwater held Addy close. "You may always be sad about him," said Stillwater. "Only time can make the hurt less . . .

". . . And while you can't see him the way you once did, he has not really gone away.

"He is in your heart. And he always will be."

Author's Note

The story of Kisa Gotami, sometimes called "The Mustard Seed," is a well-known Buddhist legend, as well as a much-loved teaching story in Buddhism. It's in a collection of the Buddha's sayings called the Dhammapada (possibly from the first century BCE, but it is likely much older still).

Kisa Gotami was a girl living at the time of the Buddha. She grew up, married, and started a family, but tragedy struck, and her son died in infancy. Having lost her only child, she was beside herself with grief. While searching for help, she was led to the Buddha.

The Buddha told her he knew of a medicine that could help her, but she would have to get it herself. He sent her out to find a single mustard seed from a home where no one had died. Kisa Gotami went from house to house searching. And when she discovered that no one is free from mortality, she was able to accept her child's death.

I have always felt that the image of death isn't a skull, but the face of a clock. The thing we all share, beyond any beliefs, is the sadness that comes from wishing for more time with our loved ones.

Death is an important aspect of life. It walks with us, hand in hand, every day. It has visited every house on every street. It is the limiter that gives each moment of our lives meaning. This is a difficult thought to consider no matter what your age.

But this wisdom is only as valuable as the compassion with which we impart it.

The most we can do in comforting someone who is grieving is to be there with them, to hear them, to acknowledge their pain.

Addy's Cup of Sugar expands the story of "The Mustard Seed." Kisa Gotami learned mortality and loss are not unique. Addy *also* discovers that what *is* unique is the time she had with her beloved kitten. Those moments will resonate throughout her life.